Blessings!
Bobbie Wright

CHRISTMAS CONSIGNMENT

BY

BOBBIE WRIGHT

ILLUSTRATED BY

STEVE FERCHAUD

A STORY FOR ALL AGES

Copyright © 2009 Bobbie Wright

All rights reserved.

ISBN: I-4392-5242-4
ISBN-I3: 9781439252420

Visit www.booksurge.com to order additional copies.

This book is dedicated to my children, grand-children, and great-grand-children. You are bright stars who have given me nothing but joy during my sojourn on earth. And to all my other "angels" in this world and the next. How could I have lived here without you?

"I had a magic moment when I was

seven years old,

but I forgot about it until…"

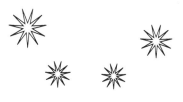

I

I was seven years old in 1931, and we lived next door to a three-story wooden house with a big porch, tall narrow windows and a high tower. Mom called it "The Victorian".

I laughed when she told me it was named for Queen Victoria because I knew a queen didn't live there. My gray-haired Aunt Amanda did. Two friends, Drucilla and Sarah, lived with her.

I knew they liked me because they gave me ginger cookies and iced lemonade in the summer and hot chocolate in the winter when the snow was deep and cold.

I was reading the Sunday funny papers after church one day when I heard Mom tell Dad she thought The Victorian was "running down". I'd never seen a house run, so I listened carefully.

"Yeah, things are really going to pot," Dad said. "The roof needs new shingles and the paint's peeling. I'll go over and help when I get a chance."

But Dad worked at the filling station and didn't get home until after dark most nights. Then he always seemed tired.

The next morning I *really* looked at the old house. Broken windows in the attic were covered with cardboard, the porch railing sagged, even the

doorbell didn't work. I had to pound on the door before Aunt Amanda heard me and let me in.

"Dad says your house is going to pot. Can I help you fix it?"

She smiled. "That's real nice of you, Andy. We've been praying for someone to help."

She called in a loud voice, "Dru and Sarah, Andy's come to fix things. Let's have tea and talk about what he can do."

Drucilla was the cook, so she put the tea kettle on the big iron claw-footed stove. Sarah took gingersnaps from the cookie jar. Aunt Amanda arranged mugs and plates and spoons precisely on the big oak table.

I climbed up on a high wooden stool and Aunt Amanda poured me a glass of milk. Drucilla said, "Take two cookies, Andy. I like to see a boy eat."

The gingersnap was so good I almost forgot what I came for, but words like "roof" and "plumbing" and "money" caught my attention. I put my cookie down and listened.

Drucilla said, "There's all kinds of things in the attic. We could start with them."

Sara replied, "The basement's full, too."

Amanda added, "We could sort through the boxes. We don't use most of my father's tools or mother's Haviland china. There's pots and pans, old clothes, even *National Geographics* magazines that go back to 1917. Everyone likes old things."

"We might find a fortune," Sarah laughed, but then suddenly frowned. "But who'll collect the money? I don't count very well."

"I'm good at numbers," Amanda said, "so I can take in the money and keep the records."

She turned to Drucilla. "You're the cook, Dru, so you don't need to help unless you want to."

"I'll help when I can."

"All right. And Sarah, do you want to arrange the tables and keep everything dusted and clean?"

Sarah beamed, "I'd like that."

Then Aunt Amanda turned to me. "Well, it's all decided, Andy. We're going to start a **'consignment shop'** in the house."

I must have looked puzzled because she explained, "A consignment shop is a store where people bring things they want to sell, like books and dishes and toys they don't use. Would you like that?"

The thought of a toy store next door made me grin. "Sure would!"

Drucilla handed me another cookie. With my mouth full, I mumbled, "Can I help, too?"

Aunt Amanda shook her head, "Don't talk with your mouth full, Andy." Then she added, "I'm not sure what you could do, dear."

"I could make sure all the toys work."

Amanda chuckled. "That's just what we need, Andy."

So it was agreed that whenever I wasn't in school, I'd be the "official toy tester" in the toy department of the Walnut Avenue Consignment Shop at a salary of two cents a day. I didn't know it, but my "Magic Moment" was about to begin.

2

The Consignment Shop opened in late summer. The ladies brought tables and chairs down from the attic, and saws and screwdrivers up from the basement. It took a whole month to sort out the boxes of books, picture frames, dishes, tools, old dresses and hats.

I'd never seen so much "junk", as my dad called it, but he painted a sign and I helped him hang it on the front of The Victorian. It said, "Walnut Street Consignment Shop." Then he fixed the doorbell, and the porch railing.

I inspected the toys. There were old iron penny banks and trucks, anagrams, a wooden rocking horse and toy soldiers. I was excited when I found toy handcuffs and a Dick Tracy badge, but I dropped those for the leather holster with a clicker gun. I pretended I was the Lone Ranger on my great white horse, Silver, until Dad told me to tend to business.

So I inspected all the trains and tractors, bats and mitts, counted all the cards, even tried out the harmonica. Aunt Amanda insisted I check everything—including dolls.

When people asked, "What do you take?" and "How much do you charge?" Amanda always answered the same way.

"We charge twenty-five percent. You set the price. We like dishes, silver, jewelry, pictures, tools, toys and games, pots and pans. We especially want **old unusual things.**"

At six o'clock, Amanda locked the door. I flipped the OPEN sign to CLOSED, and Drucilla and Sarah pulled the shades down before we all sat at the kitchen table and counted the money.

They were pleased. Amanda gave me my two pennies for "testing toys", and then she stuffed the rest of the cash into a canning jar before putting it on the highest shelf in the kitchen.

Aunt Amanda walked me to the door.

My eyes went to the shiny red and black dump truck on the floor. It cost fifty cents. I shoved the pennies into my pocket, bent over and patted the truck. "I hope no one buys you," I said.

Amanda unlocked the door. "Good night, Andy. Come again tomorrow. You're a good helper."

The next few weeks went fast. I counted every checker and tiddlywink that came in the door. There were metal racing cars and motorcycles, and card games like Old Maid, Rook, Fish and Flint. I tested the toy drum until Aunt Amanda asked me to stop.

When I didn't know how to check things like pinochle decks or ice skates, my dad okayed them. Dolls and teddy bears were easy. If they had an eye or a leg missing, I told Sarah. She tied on a special "As Is" tag.

My dump truck didn't sell, and I kept saving my pennies, but I felt uneasy about that truck. I felt sure someone else was going to buy it.

3

After school started I couldn't work much, but I still checked on the truck every afternoon. The first snowfall made everything look different and the three old ladies started humming Christmas carols. They filled the house with sweet-smelling pine boughs and red ribbons. Then they put a big Christmas tree in the dining room, decorating it with old glass ornaments and tinsel.

I had a strange tingly feeling, like we were preparing for something **GREAT** to happen. But

I know the three ladies were not prepared for the old man who wandered in late one afternoon, just before dusk.

I was testing a jack-in-the-box on the floor. Snow was falling and the shop was crowded with people looking for gifts. The white-haired man spent an hour slowly examining almost everything in the shop.

Amanda's eyes followed him. "He's clean," she told Drucilla, "and his hair's cut. He even shaved this morning."

"But he's not buying anything." Drucilla had come from the kitchen wiping her hands on her ample apron. "Maybe he steals," she whispered.

I could see Amanda watching him more carefully after that. He picked up an old blue bottle, put it down carefully, and then tried on a black felt hat.

"He's too old to be working," she murmured to Sarah. "Maybe he just needs a place to keep warm." I knew she didn't mean to be unkind, but she added, "Then he can just go to the library."

At six o'clock she reversed the OPEN sign. Sarah started cleaning up the tables. I smelled pot roast when Drucilla came out of the kitchen to help.

Customers made last minute purchases and left. I played with my dump truck on the floor. When everyone had gone, the old man stood shifting from one foot to the other.

Finally he cleared his throat. "Ahem, I was wonderin'..."

Aunt Amanda shoved her hands deep into the sagging pockets of her old beige sweater. Her face looked pinched.

He looked at the floor, then ran his finger along an oak table as if checking for dust, before asking, "You take things on consignment?"

"Yes, we take..." and Aunt Amanda recited her list.

"You mentioned **old unusual things.** That's what I'm wonderin'. Would you take **ME**?"

I stopped playing with the truck and I could see Sarah and Drucilla listening closely. Amanda frowned. "I don't understand."

"Well, I'm old and kind of unusual!"

"But how would we *sell* you?" Amanda's lips pursed tightly. "We have to make money."

"I have money," he said. He pulled out a bankbook and showed her the amount.

Amanda shook her head, " No, it wouldn't be right, mister. I think you'd better leave."

But Sarah said softly, "Let's hear what he has to say, Amanda."

The old man rushed ahead. "My name's Jack Ryder. I used to live in this town years ago. I've traveled all over the world, but now I want to settle down. I'd like a nice woman who cooks good and has a warm home. So I want to be consigned to your shop."

He added, "I'll make you out a check for a hundred dollars for a month's board and room. If some woman doesn't take me up on my offer, I'll just move on. I'm used to doin' that."

Amanda's face still looked tight.

But Sarah smiled. I knew she liked him.

Drucilla said, "Why don't you stay to supper, Mr. Ryder, and we can talk about it?"

She added. "There's pot roast simmering on the stove and fresh baked bread. Made it myself this morning."

Mr. Ryder beamed. He turned to Aunt Amanda. "That all right with you, lady?"

Amanda sniffed. "My name's Amanda and this is Sara and the cook is Drucilla. If she invited you, you're invited."

I followed them into the warm kitchen, hoping they'd invite me to dinner, too. I could tell Amanda was nervous by the way she picked up dishes and set them down again quickly. She showed Mr. Ryder where to wash up in the hall bathroom.

"You wash your hands here in the kitchen, Andy, and I'll call your mother to see if you can stay."

I knew Mom would say yes.

The ladies whispered among themselves while he was gone.

"...we could sure use the money."

"...it would only be for a month."

"...but what would the neighbors think?"

We sat down silently at the table. Mr. Ryder ate pot roast, potatoes and carrots, lots of bread and butter and then politely asked for more, praising Drucilla's cooking.

Amanda watched him like a hawk but finally said, "That argyle vest you're wearing reminds me of one Papa wore." She sounded softer.

When he'd finished his second piece of blackberry pie, Mr. Ryder leaned back, wiped his mouth with his napkin and said, "Your faucet's drippin'. I can fix that."

"Are you a plumber?" Amanda always needed a plumber.

"No, ma'am, but I can fix 'most anything. It just needs a new washer. Got my tools back at the hotel."

He paused, finishing his coffee, wiping his mouth with his napkin. "So what do ya' think?"

Amanda seemed unwilling to rush. "Could you come back in the morning? We need to talk about it."

Sarah spoke up, her soft voice unusually firm, "I'm ready right now. If Mr. Ryder can fix the plumbing around here, that's enough for me."

Even Drucilla liked the idea. "Just think what we can do with the money, Amanda! The lace curtains can be replaced, and with all the people coming and going, the front door is almost falling off its hinges."

"I can fix that," Mr. Ryder said.

All three ladies stared at him. Amanda spoke first. "Then it's settled...if you like the room, that is."

They ushered him up the stairs into the tower, giggling like girls at school.

I followed silently. They'd forgotten about me.

Mr. Ryder walked over to the tower window and pulled the white lace curtains aside, looking out on Walnut Street. Then he sat down on the white iron bedstead and tested the mattress. He looked around at the mahogany bureau and shabby brown rug.

"Room's fine," he said. "Can I move in tonight? I'd like to get settled."

Amanda seemed surprised. She looked at Sarah and Drucilla. They nodded their heads silently. Mr. Ryder pulled out his checkbook and wrote them a check.

While he was gone to get his belongings, Sarah and Amanda opened the window to air out the room. They put clean sheets on the bed. Drucilla laid fresh tissue paper in the bureau drawers.

I watched out the window. "He's coming," I called.

We all met him at the door. Mr. Ryder returned with a brown leather satchel and a scarred wooden toolbox with the initials "J.R." carved roughly into the side.

"That's all you have?" Amanda seemed curious.

"Yep, I travel light."

I followed them back upstairs.

"We hope the room's fine, Mr. Ryder." Amanda still looked worried.   "There's fresh towels in the bathroom and if you need anything else, just let us know."

Aunt Amanda finally noticed me.   "My goodness, Andy, your mother will be worried. You'd better scoot home."

I said good night. As I left I touched my truck for luck on the way out. I had dreams about that truck. So far, no one had bought it.

4

The next day was Saturday. I bundled up early to go to my job. The sky was bright blue and the brilliant sun shining on the snow almost blinded me as I hurried across the lot to The Victorian.

The kitchen was filled with odors of ham and eggs and hotcakes with maple syrup. Drucilla gave me a pancake. I'd already had corn flakes at home, but I ate it anyway as I watched Mr. Ryder eat.

Drucilla smiled all over when he finally leaned back, wiped his mouth with his napkin and said, "Best pancakes I've ever eaten!"

But Amanda wanted to get things settled quickly. "Now, how shall we 'sell' you, Mr. Ryder?"

"I thought about it last night," he said. "How about a sign?"

Sarah brought cardboard, a black crayon and a ball of twine.

Mr. Ryder carefully printed:

"WANTED: Gentle single lady to take me home. No charge. I'm kind and can fix almost anything. In return I'd like good cooking, a happy home, and a yellow dog. Dog not necessary."

Attaching the twine, he hung the sign around his neck.

"There. How's that?" he asked.

"That...that should do it, Mr. Ryder," Sarah stammered, "if...if anyone's looking."

"Now, where should I sit?"

"Over by the tree, I think," Drucilla replied. "You'll make some woman a good Christmas present."

But I knew Amanda was still suspicious when she asked, "What about the kitchen faucet and the front door?"

"I'll get my tools. Anything else needs fixin', just make me a list. Got time on my hands now." He seemed happy.

The old man left his sign on the brown chair, whistling as he put on his tool belt. Then he winked at Sarah, who blushed again.

The shop was soon busy, but when Amanda and I had a sandwich at noon, Drucilla told her the faucet was fixed.

When Mr. Ryder asked me if I wanted to help him fix the front door, I nodded.

He took his tool box and said, "Then you can hold these hinges for me."

The door was fixed almost before Amanda realized what we were doing. Then he put his sign back on and sat in the chair eating a turkey sandwich Drucilla brought him for lunch.

"Humph! We'll never 'sell' him," I heard Amanda whisper to Sarah as she sat primly behind the antique cash register her father had owned when his feed store went "belly up". I wasn't sure what that meant, but Dad said a lot of stores were doing that in the Depression we were in.

But Mr. Ryder sat quietly, eating his sandwich, watching the ladies who came into the shop.

Some of the women never glanced his way, but others eyed the white-haired man carefully, reading the sign and laughing. "Wish I could take you home," one woman said. "I'd trade my husband for you if you could fix my furnace."

Another woman came back twice to read the sign. She stared at Mr. Ryder, got red in the face, then shook her head and ran out of the shop without buying anything.

"She's thinkin' about it," the old man laughed. "Maybe she'll be back."

But by six o'clock no one had taken him up on his offer. Before I left I heard Sarah say, "He fixed the door good, and the faucet, too. I like him. He's not underfoot all the time, doesn't even smoke."

Amanda said, "I thought that woman might come back for him."

"It's a big step," Drucilla commented. "Like pickin' out a dog. You gotta be careful."

They seemed very pleased with Mr. Ryder. Aunt Amanda liked it because the door and faucet were fixed, and she gave him a list of a dozen more repairs he could do. Sarah was happy helping someone, and Drucilla enjoyed his compliments about her cooking.

Amanda was the first to voice the thought, "Perhaps we should keep him."

"But he only wants one woman, not three," Drucilla stated firmly. "My husband, Al, was a one-woman man."

Sarah just smiled sweetly.

5

I was sad when my dump truck disappeared just before Christmas vacation. Someone must have bought it.

When no new toys arrived, Mr. Ryder showed me how to build a fire in the fireplace and how to hammer nails. Later he and I repaired the tile floor in the bathroom. One day we fixed three broken windows in the attic.

Many women looked Mr. Ryder over. Some came back two or three times. One large woman in a dark blue coat cornered Amanda, asking a lot of questions, but she seemed too flustered to approach Mr. Ryder on her own.

"Perhaps it's just because it's Christmas—so much shopping and cooking to do. After the new year..." Amanda comforted him.

We all spent time shopping and wrapping presents, even Mr. Ryder. I'd saved all my pennies, and Mom helped me wrap five cent Baby Ruth candy bars. I sneaked them under the tree when no one was looking.

The shop closed early on Christmas Eve. Mom said I could stay and exchange presents. Drucilla cooked pork chops with mashed potatoes and gravy, green beans and a delicious cherry cake.

After dinner we pulled chairs into the dining room and sat before the twinkling lights of the Christmas tree listening to "Silent Night" on the radio.

That excited tingling feeling came over me again. My feet wouldn't keep still and I kept patting my legs. I felt so jumpy I could hardly stay in the chair.

Then we presented our gifts. I was first, and my Baby Ruth's were opened, tasted, and declared "delicious".

Aunt Amanda gave wool scarves and mittens to everyone. Mine were blue.

Sarah gave her friends bottles of their favorite perfumes, and me a toy cash register for my pennies. She blushed when she gave something called "Bay Rum Aftershave" to Mr. Ryder.

He opened the bottle, sniffed, and then patted some aftershave on his face. "I smell good. Perhaps some woman will buy me now." And he laughed.

Sarah blushed even more.

Drucilla's gifts were books—*Huckleberry Finn* for me and a travel book with pictures of Africa for Mr. Ryder.

He was obviously pleased. "I've been there," he said, examining the pages. "It takes me back. Thanks."

Drucilla beamed.

I watched Mr. Ryder present his packages. Amanda opened hers first, a silver pin with purple stones. She smiled with pleasure and pinned it on her green housedress.

He gave Sarah a soft pink sweater that matched her cheeks and brought out the blue of her eyes. The ladies *oohed* when she held it up. Sarah's cheeks turned almost bright red.

Finally Drucilla opened her gift, a small gold-framed painting of fruit on a silver platter. "Oh, you shouldn't have," she protested.

"I'll always remember your wonderful meals," Mr. Ryder said. "Even if some nice woman comes along, I'll bet she can't cook like you."

Drucilla grinned and held the picture against the wall. "I'll hang it in my room and think of you every time I see it."

She walked over and kissed Mr. Ryder on his cheek. Amanda laughed in embarrassment.

Then Sarah gave him a kiss, too. Not to be outdone, Amanda finally stood and added a quick peck on his forehead.

"I'm tired," she said. "Think I'll go to bed."

"Wait a minute. There's one more gift." Mr. Ryder climbed the stairs, returning with a large box wrapped in green tissue paper. "This is for my helper, Andy."

I ripped the box open. Inside was my wonderful red and black dump truck. I couldn't believe my eyes. I knew it had been sold, but I didn't know he'd bought it for *me*.

"Oh, thanks, Mr. Ryder. I really wanted this truck."

"I know, Andy," he said. "I watched your eyes light up every time you looked at it."

I hugged him, then hugged all the ladies.

Drucilla said, "It's been such a *nice* Christmas."

Amanda turned out the lights on the Christmas tree, Sarah turned off the radio, and Mr. Ryder said he'd help me carry my presents home.

I still felt tingly.

6

I held my truck and Mr. Ryder carried everything else. Outside the stars were sparkling in a clear dark sky and the air was so crisp and cold it made my eyes water. He took my hand going down the icy steps. Then he let go.

"I want to thank you, Andy, for all the help you gave me in the house. You're a good worker. This old world needs lots of helpers," he said.

The tingly feeling kept growing, becoming almost unbearable, like something inside of me was itching, trying to get out of my skin.

I looked up at Mr. Ryder. His face was shining, kind of glowing, and his white hair sparkled in the faint moonlight.

"Did you ever see such stars, Andy?" He pointed upward. "The ancient ones called those three in a line, 'Orion's Belt.' And see, they point to the brightest star in the whole sky. It's called 'Sirius.' Always head for the brightest light, Andy."

I stared at the brilliant star.

Almost instantly my feet left the earth and I felt drawn up into the dark night—planets and stars seemed to be rushing by. I was frightened until I saw Mr. Ryder zooming along beside me.

He smiled and took my hand. "Just enjoy the ride, Andy," he said.

We headed for the brightest star in front of us. Earth became a tiny speck in the blackness of space, but I wasn't afraid. The tingly feeling was replaced by something that bounced in my stomach like a ping-pong ball.

I smiled as we flew by Venus, and chuckled as we zoomed by Mars.

Mr. Ryder laughed, too, as we turned cartwheels on the rings of Saturn. This was more exciting than any circus.

Passing beyond the Milky Way galaxy, we twirled around huge nebulas full of glowing gases. The feeling inside me kept growing, bubbling and bouncing around, just like I was.

We danced on strange planets, hopped up and down on unknown stars, rode imaginary horses on suns whose solar flares never burned us.

As we skipped through the cosmos hand in hand, the universe became a huge playground and

I frolicked and reveled in all of it. Then the wonder of it all overcame me. I slowed down, took a deep breath, and stared at comets silently passing on their immense journeys through space, at distant black holes, giant red stars, novas and super galaxies.

The feeling inside me rose higher and higher, reaching my eyes, making me lightheaded and dizzy. Almost over-whelmed, I saw the universe differently. Dropping Mr. Ryder's hand, I spread my arms wide in awe.

The celestial heavens were open and I knew the universe was my true home. I'd always known it. I was only visiting earth for a while.

Then I heard my mother call my name…

Instantly I was standing on the frozen snow in front of my house. The tingly feeling was gone. Mr. Ryder stood beside me holding my

presents. My dump truck was in my arms. The glow around the old man's head had disappeared and I was cold.

I watched Mother walk toward us. She said, "Merry Christmas, Mr. Ryder," as he handed her my presents.

The stars twinkled far above us, beckoning me to remember. I smiled as I stared at Sirius. I didn't think I'd ever forget my journey through space looking for the brightest star. Mom took my hand and we walked quietly into the house, where soft colored Christmas tree lights shone on Dad sitting in his favorite old chair. All the presents were piled underneath the tree. Dad looked up from his paper and smiled. "Have a good Christmas Eve, Andy?"

My mind was so jumbled I could only nod my head as I held out the dump truck.

"That's great. But tomorrow's a big day, you'd better get to bed."

I turned and waved to Mr. Ryder. He nodded and smiled, then walked slowly back to the Consignment Shop.

7

The next morning I yelled "Merry Christmas" as I flew out of my bedroom, expecting stockings and presents and candy, but Mom and Dad stood quietly whispering as they looked out at the snow-covered street. Dad put his arm around me.

A police car was parked at the curb in front of the consignment shop and two officers were knocking on Aunt Amanda's front door.

"What's wrong, Dad?"

"We don't know, Andy. Maybe you'd better get dressed."

In my room I pulled on my overalls, boots and jacket, but Dad was gone by the time I finished. I raced across the snow and up the steps of The Victorian.

The front door was open. When I heard people talking in the tower, I climbed the stairs.

The two policemen stood in the bedroom. Dad pinned me gently to his side, but I could see between the officers.

Mr. Ryder was lying on the bed with his eyes closed. He had a little smile on his face, just like when he handed me my dump truck. Dad squeezed me hard, and I didn't cry.

One of the policemen said, "Looks like his heart just stopped beating. Who found him?"

The three ladies had their arms around each other. With tears in her eyes, Aunt Amanda replied, "We all did. When he didn't come down for breakfast, we came up to get him."

Sarah said, "He was such a good man," and she started to cry.

Drucilla added, "I loved to see him eat."

"What's his name?" The policeman had his pad and pen out, taking notes.

"Jack Ryder," Aunt Amanda replied.

"Is he related to one of you?"

"No, he just wandered in a few weeks ago."

"What do you mean, 'wandered in'?" The officer was puzzled.

Amanda struggled to explain. "He came in trying to find a good home with a kind lady. We took him in until we could sort of …" Amanda searched for words… "*sell* him."

"Sell him?" The young officer wrinkled his brow. "What do you mean?"

"He gave us a hundred dollars for board and room. Here's the sign he made. That's all we know, officer."

The policeman stared at the hand-printed sign with the twine sagging limply:

"WANTED: Gentle, single lady to take me home. No charge. I'm kind and can fix almost anything. In return I'd like good cooking, a happy home, and a yellow dog. Dog not necessary."

"I never heard anything like this before."

Drucilla spoke up. "We hadn't either, officer. But he was such a good man. He fixed everything in the house—the faucet, the front door, the floor in the bathroom..."

Amanda continued, "And the washing machine, the broken windows, and the kitchen tiles. He came just when we needed him. He was a god-send!"

Sarah's eyes widened and sparkled with a sudden flash of awareness. She looked slowly around at each of the ladies.

"Of course. Don't you see?"

Everyone stared at her, not understanding what she meant.

"It's so clear to me." She smiled in her soft gentle way. "We prayed for help, and Mr. Ryder came. He fixed *everything.* He was an answer to our prayers."

She turned and looked down at the old man lying peacefully on the bed and added, "Then he went back home. He was truly an *ANGEL ON CONSIGNMENT.*"

Afterward

I suppose the shock of the old man's death covered up the memory of my "Magic Moment". When I was 18, I was drafted and served in Europe in World War II. I was wounded in France and received the Purple Heart medal.

Aunt Amanda passed away while I was recovering in the hospital. Sarah married a man she met in the Consignment Shop, and Drucilla went to live with her daughter.

My mother wrote that Amanda left The Victorian to me in her will, since I'd helped repair it so many times. I went to college on the GI Bill and when I graduated I started teaching high school science. I moved into the old house.

At night I'd sometimes sit on the front porch and watch the stars. When I set up a telescope in the back yard, kids came and looked through it, learning about comets, and constellations and galaxies.

I married Susan, my high school sweetheart. A few years later we had a baby boy we named John. We also acquired a big yellow dog we called Tag.

We kept the tower room for guests—kids having a rough time at home, or an occasional tramp who came to the door looking for a handout. You could do that in those days.

Drucilla called me occasionally to repair a leak in her daughter's kitchen, and Mom always needed her screens taken down in the fall and replaced in the spring. I liked helping.

One Saturday, when my son was seven, we were in the basement looking for washers for the bathroom faucet, which was leaking again.

John crawled behind some ladders and paint cans, dragging out an old scarred toolbox with the initials "J.R." carved into the side. I sat down on the step and stared at it.

A familiar feeling came over me, that same kind of excited rush I always get at Christmas, like something **GREAT** *is going to happen. It started at my toes and ran up to my scalp.*

The old man, Jack Ryder, suddenly appeared in front of me, smiling just like he did that night in the snow in front of my house when I was seven years old. The same glow surrounded him, and his white hair sparkled.

Shocked, I said, "I thought you were dead, Mr. Ryder."

"No one ever dies, Andy," he replied. "Don't you remember what I told you?"

Memories began to return—the joy and awe of that starry night long ago.

"I remember you told me to 'look for the brightest light'."

As I spoke those words, I felt myself lifting up again, flying through the skies with the kind old man, laughing joyously as the heavens opened.

We danced on strange planets, hopped up and down on unknown stars, rode imaginary horses on suns whose solar flares never burned us. I was a child again and the entire universe was my playground.

"I had to come back to help you remember, Andy."

Mr. Ryder grinned at me. "And to tell you that you and the universe are one energy . And you are never separate from the universe. So when you think you're dying, always head for the brightest light. It will never fail you."

I turned to stare at the tremendous universe, and I knew what he meant. There'd always be a brighter light beckoning me. And the entire universe was my home.

But when I turned back, Mr. Ryder was nowhere to be seen. I was in the basement again, and my son John was exploring the toolbox, pulling out hammers and pliers, screwdrivers and wrenches I'd seen the old man use.

"Would you like to have that toolbox, John?" I asked.

His smile was all the answer I needed.

"Then it's yours. It belonged to an old man I once knew. He'd like you to have it."

I seemed to hear Mr. Ryder's words echoing through the house. "This old world needs lots of helpers."

"You can be a helper like he was, John." I said.

My son started to pound a nail into a board and I showed him how to hold the hammer correctly, just as Jack Ryder had once shown me. Then I said

"You may have a
'Magic Moment'
this year, John, and it may be
so wonderful, so unusual, you might
not believe it's real…"

There's Never An End

Aunt Amanda's Gingersnaps

Sift together two times:
- 2 cups flour
- 1 Tbs. ground ginger
- 2 tsp. baking powder
- 1 tsp. cinnamon
- ½ tsp. salt

In separate bowl, cream together
- ¾ cup shortening
- 1 cup sugar, added gradually

Then beat in
- 1 egg
- 1 cup dark molasses

Add flour mixture to sugar mixture

Roll into small balls (about 1 Tbs.) and dip in granulated sugar. Bake on ungreased cookie sheet at 350 degrees for 12–15 minutes. Cool on rack, then enjoy.

A Note from the Author

My Magic Moment came when I was 52 years old. As I was going to sleep one night, I heard a distinct voice in my head saying, "I am entering you." I had been asking for spiritual guides to assist me in my life, but I wanted to make sure nothing bad would happen, so I replied, "Only if it's for good." Then I turned over and calmly went to sleep.

Later that night I awoke, feeling as if someone were trying to communicate with me. Without waking my husband, I went into the family room and set up my tape recorder. It's hard to explain the great feeling that enveloped me. When my husband came into the room about an hour later I felt he should be able to see the aura of love surrounding me.

The voice said he could be called David, but that names were unnecessary. And that my name was Calliope, and that we had been together many times in past lives. I asked many questions, and I'm still asking them today.

This was my Magic Moment, and it resulted in awesome changes for me, my loving husband, and my friends and family.

Have you had a Magic Moment? It might have come at any time of your life. Andy's Magic Moment came when he was seven. Like him, perhaps I forgot my childhood experience and had to wait nearly half a century for another one.

I would like to hear from you regarding your Magic Moment. Email me at xmas1931@ yahoo.com and tell me your story. I'm collecting these for a "Magic Moment" book that could enlarge human awareness. We are so much more than we think we are.

And thank you for reading my story. It was given me in love. I hope you enjoyed it and will read it for many Christmases to come.

Bobbie Wright, 2009

P.S. If you enjoy the creative illustrations in this book, they were drawn by Steve Ferchaud, a good friend of mine. You can contact him at www.steveferchaud.com and view more of his wonderful work.

Write about your own "Magic Moment" here:

Write about your own Magic Moment here:

4108207

Made in the USA
Charleston, SC
01 December 2009